OF ALL PLACES: THE ENCORE!

PERCY'S 5TH TREEHOUSE - 2025

PERCY WAS ON THE BALCONY IN HIS TREEHOUSE LOOKING AT THE SUBURBS AND PALM TREE'S AROUND

HE WAS THINKING BACK TO 10 YEARS AGO AND WAS WISHING

I SHOULD HAVE JUST, COME CLEAN

PALM TREE ISLAND - FLORIDA (10 YEARS EARLIER)

WOOOOOOO!!!!!!

HOW YA'LL DOING TODAY YOU GOOD?

WOOO!

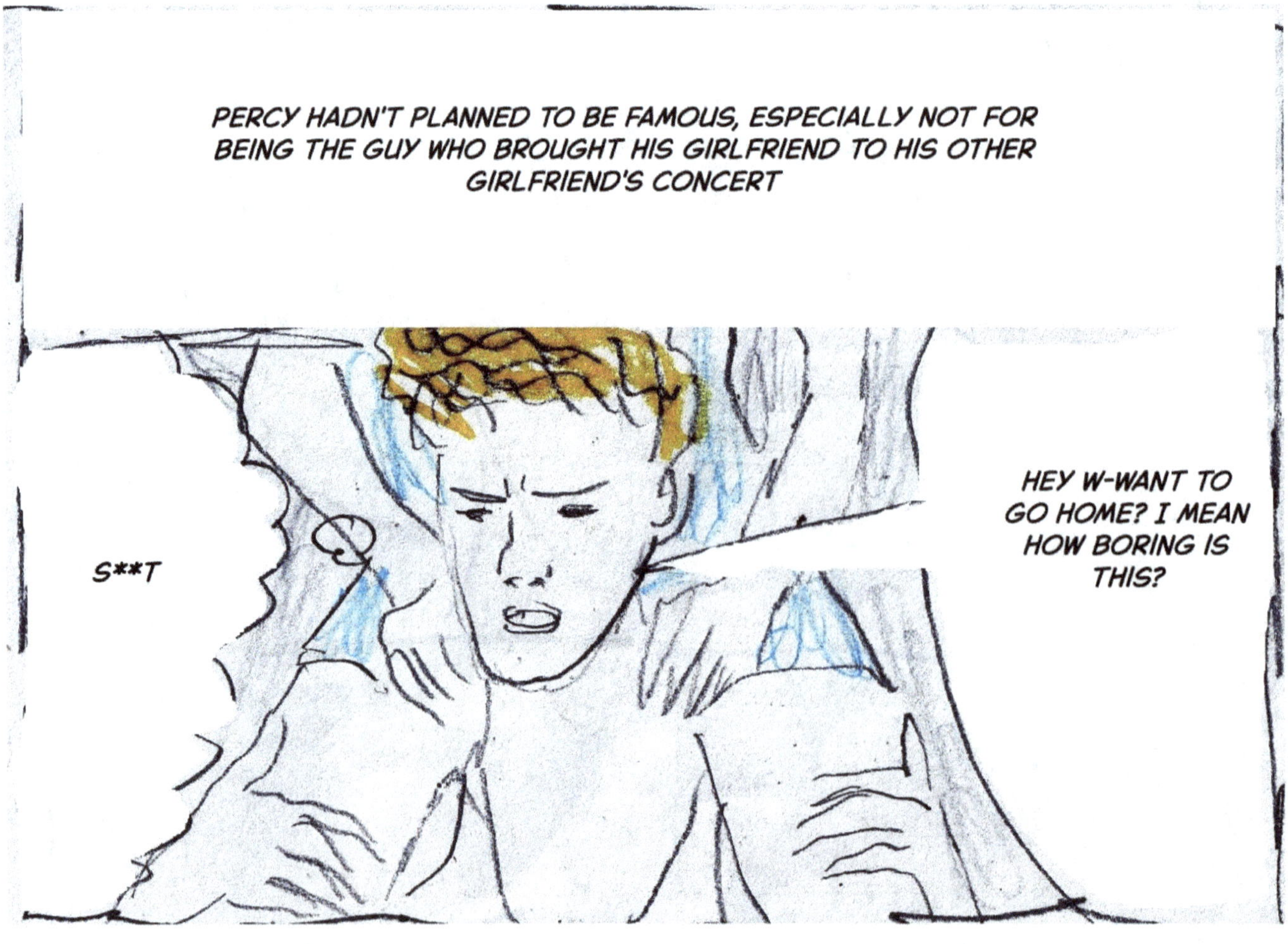

PERCY HADN'T PLANNED TO BE FAMOUS, ESPECIALLY NOT FOR BEING THE GUY WHO BROUGHT HIS GIRLFRIEND TO HIS OTHER GIRLFRIEND'S CONCERT

S**T

HEY W-WANT TO GO HOME? I MEAN HOW BORING IS THIS?

IT HAD BEEN THREE WEEKS SINCE PAMELA TRILL'S SHOW, WHERE PERCY BROUGHT SHAYLEE

YEAH I'M SCREWED

THE FALLOUT WAS BRUTAL: VIRAL VIDEOS

MEMES, ONE OF WHICH SAID "HOW I PICTURE MY BOYFRIEND WHEN HE SAYS HE'S FAITHFUL (AND IT HAD A PICTURE OF PERCY)

AND A TRENDING HASHTAG ON BLUEBOOK CALLED #PERCYTHETWOTIMER

IT WAS NIGHT TIME NOW AND PERCY WAS IN HIDING IN HIS COUSIN'S GARAGE

HE HADN'T SPOKEN TO EITHER GIRL SINCE.....HE WAS THINKING ON WHAT TO SAY BUT SUDDENLY HIS

PERCY SAT CROSSED LEGGED ON A STAINED MATTRESS IN HIS COUSIN'S GARAGE, THE STONE WALLS REMINDED HIM OF WHEN HE WAS IN SOLIDARY CONFINEMENT. THE PLACE SMELLED LIKE CARDBOARD, MOTOR OIL AND REGRET

HIS ORANGE ARMOUR - DENTED, DUSTY AND HALF DISASSEMBLED (WITH NANOBOTS SCATTERED ACROSS THE MATTRESS) - LEANED AGAINST A STACK OF CARDBOARD BOXES, LIKE A FALLEN IDOL THAT BROKE CARRYING THE WORLD ON IT'S SHOULDERS. HE HADN'T TOUCHED IT IN WEEKS, HE WAS SCARED WHAT HE WOULD TO DO TO HIS MILLIONS OF HATERS

THREE DAYS

SAID TOBIN AS HE STOOD IN THE DOORWAY FROM THE GARAGE TO THE MAIN HOUSE

THEN I WANT YOU GONE

YOU SAID THAT LAST WEEK

YEAH AND I MEANT IT THEN TOO BUT NOW I REALLY MEAN IT

I'M SERIOUS COUSIN

TOBIN WAS 30, WORKED NIGHTS AT A WAREHOUSE, AND HAD A FACE THAT LOOKED LIKE IT HAD FORGOTTEN HOW TO SMILE, HE'S LET PERCY CRASH IN THE GARAGE (PERCY LITERALLY FLEW PUT OF THE SKY AND CRASHED STRAIGHT INTO THE GARAGE WITH THE ORANGE ARMOUR ON) AFTER THE SCANDAL BROKE OUT- AFTER THE CONCERT, THE CHEATING, THE VIRAL FOOTAGE, THE UNMASKING. THE WORLD HAD LOVED ORANGE ARMOUR, UNTIL THEY SAW PERCY RUNNING OFF LIKE A COWARD WHEN PRESENTED WITH THE CHOICE ON WHEVER TO SAVE PAMELA OR SHAYLEE

You know what your problem is? You think being smart gives you a free pass to being an ass

It was one mistake!

I saved people man! I stopped a tram derailing, I kicked the st out of Smirkgown when he mangled that theatre into a ball and hung it over the ocean, I took down a giant Zintendo SD system and took down the walking fever dream that came out of it! I-**

SILENCE HUNG BETWEEN THEM, OUTSIDE A DOG BARKED, A CAR PASSED. INSIDE THE GARAGE PERCY'S ORANGE ARMOUR CAUGHT LIGHT - ORANGE, BOLD, AND <u>BROKEN</u>

YOU KNOW WHAT THIS THING IS? IT'S A MIRROR AND RIGHT NOW IT'S SHOWING YOU EXACTLY WHO YOU ARE

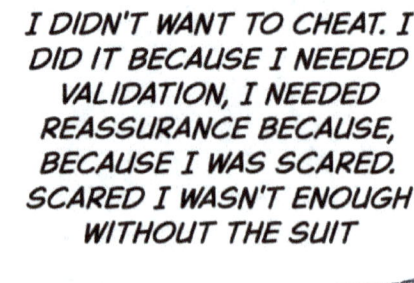

I DIDN'T WANT TO CHEAT. I DID IT BECAUSE I NEEDED VALIDATION, I NEEDED REASSURANCE BECAUSE, BECAUSE I WAS SCARED. SCARED I WASN'T ENOUGH WITHOUT THE SUIT

SCARED THEY'D FIND OUT I WAS JUST A KID WITH A BIG MOUTH AND A BUSTED HEART

BUT LITTLE DID PERCY KNOW AS HE WALKED THROUGH THE SUBURBS

SOMEONE WAS WAITING FOR HIM WITH A GUN!!!!!!
THEY WERE WEARING A BLUE TOP...BUT WHO WERE THEY?

TO BE CONTINUED

www.ingramcontent.com/pod-product-compliance
Lightning Source LLC
LaVergne TN
LVHW061935070526
838200LV00071B/2260